First edition

Published by Ladybird Books Ltd Loughborough Leicestershire UK

Printed in England (3)

WINNIE THE POOH
Tigger in trouble

Ladybird Books

Christopher Robin and Pooh

Christopher Robin and Winnie the Pooh were best friends. They lived in a wonderful world of their own in the middle of the Forest, where grown-ups never came. It was

called the Hundred Acre Wood, and lots of other friends lived there too.

There was Piglet, Kanga and Baby Roo, Tigger, gloomy old Eeyore, Rabbit and Owl, and they all had happy times together, as well as some very unusual adventures.

Tigger and Rabbit

Of everyone who lived in the Hundred Acre Wood, the bounciest was Tigger. As Tigger himself often said, "Bouncing is what Tiggers do best!"

Tigger's bounciness was not always appreciated by his friends. Rabbit, in particular, got quite cross when Tigger bounced at him, especially if he was tending his vegetable patch at the time. Tigger always made such a mess!

Rabbit tried time and again to stop Tigger bouncing, but his plans never worked. Then, one day, Tigger discovered for himself that bouncing could be overdone.

It happened one winter morning, when the Forest was covered in snow...

Tigger and Roo

On this snowy day, Roo was sitting on his mailbox, waiting eagerly for Tigger to arrive.

"When is he going to get here, Mama?" Roo asked Kanga. "I can't wait to play in the snow!"

"Be patient, dear," said Kanga with a smile. "He'll be here – "

Before she could finish her sentence, Tigger came bouncing and pouncing through the snow. "Whee!" he laughed, as he skidded to a stop. "Well, here I am! Did I surprise you, Roo?"

"You certainly did!" said Roo

happily. "I like surprises!"

He jumped from the mailbox and landed in a pile of snow.

"Are you ready for some bouncing?" asked Tigger.

"Yes, yes!" squealed Roo. "We're very good at bouncing, aren't we, Tigger?"

"Of course we are!" said Tigger. "Bouncing is what Tiggers do best of all!"

"Now, just a moment, dear," said Kanga, as she took off her scarf and wound it round Roo's neck. "Keep this scarf on. And is your sweater warm enough?"

"Yes, Mama!" said Roo impatiently. "Can I go now, please?"

"All right," said Kanga. "Tigger, make sure you have Roo home in time for his nap. And do be careful!"

"Don't worry, Mrs Kanga," said Tigger. "I'll take care of the little nipper!"

And Tigger and Roo bounced off into the Forest.

Roo enjoyed the view as he bounced along on Tigger's shoulders. He had never seen snow before, and he thought the Hundred Acre Wood looked enchanting in its blanket of sparkling white.

There was a lake in the Forest, and Tigger decided to bounce towards that. As he and Roo came closer, they saw that the lake was frozen solid, and that Rabbit was skating along its glassy surface.

"Halloo, Long Ears!" Tigger called.

Rabbit pretended not to hear. He didn't want Tigger bouncing in and spoiling his fun.

And Rabbit especially didn't like being called "Long Ears". So he just went on gliding along the ice, smiling and humming to himself.

Tigger and Roo stood beside the lake and watched Rabbit.

"That looks like fun," said Roo. "Can Tiggers ice skate as well as Rabbits?"

"Can Tiggers ice skate?" said Tigger. "Why, that's what Tiggers do best! Just watch!" And he bounded onto the ice.

But Tigger lost his balance. He went slipping and sliding and stumbling wildly across the ice, till he crashed into Rabbit and sent them both tumbling into a snowbank.

"Why me?" groaned Rabbit, rubbing his head. "Why does it always have to be me?"

"Tiggers *don't* like ice skating!" Tigger announced, brushing the snow off his fur. "Let's look for something else to do, Roo."

"I know!" said Roo. "I'll bet you can climb trees, Tigger."

"Of course I can!" said Tigger. "In fact, Tiggers don't just climb trees, we *bounce* up them. I'll show you!"

With Roo clinging to his neck, Tigger gave a huge bounce and went shooting straight up into a tree. "That was a good bounce, wasn't it, Roo?" he said.

"Oh, yes!" cried Roo gleefully.

Tigger Bounces Higher

Tigger bounced farther and farther up the tree. "See?" he said to Roo. "I told you Tiggers could climb trees!"

Suddenly Tigger looked down. The ground seemed a long, long way below.

"Hey," Tigger gasped, "how did this tree get so *high*?"

By now Roo was feeling quite at home in the tree, and he began clambering up and down the branches on his own.

"Ooh, Tigger," he squealed, "I can't wait to tell Mama how much fun we've been having!"

"Er...ah...maybe you'd better not say anything to your mama," said Tigger, hanging on to the tree for dear life.

"Why not, Tigger?" asked Roo.

"Because," said Tigger, "even though Tiggers are very good at getting *up* trees, I'm not absolutely positively sure I can remember how to get *down*!"

"That's all right," said Roo. "I like it up here! I hope we can stay for a long, long time!"

Suddenly Roo grabbed hold of Tigger's tail and began to swing back and forth. "Ooh, this is even more fun than climbing!" he cried. He enjoyed it so much that he made up a little song:

"Don't swing on a string,
It's much too frail!
The best kind of swing
Is a Tigger's tail!"

But all the swinging was making Tigger very dizzy.

"Stop, Roo, please!" he begged. "You're rocking the Forest!"

"I'm sorry," said Roo, settling down on a nearby branch. "What's the matter, Tigger?"

"I was just getting a little seasick," said Tigger, "from...seeing too much!"

Pooh and Piglet Go Tracking

Meanwhile, down on the ground, Piglet was watching Pooh, who was staring at some paw prints in the snow.

"What are you doing, Pooh?" enquired Piglet.

"Tracking something," replied Pooh.

"What are you tracking?" asked Piglet.

"I don't know yet," said Pooh. "I'll have to wait until I catch up with it."

"Pooh," said Piglet, admiringly, "for a Bear of Very Little Brain you certainly are very clever."

Suddenly Pooh came to a halt. "Aha!" he said. "A very mysterious thing, Piglet. Look – there's a whole new set of tracks."

What Pooh hadn't realised was that he and Piglet were walking round in a circle and the paw prints they were following were their own!

And so they went on, feeling a little anxious now in case the animals in front of them were of Hostile Intent.

Suddenly, Pooh and Piglet heard a sound. A moaning, bellowing, howling sort of sound. They stopped and listened.

"*Hallooooo*," they heard.

"There's something in that tree over there," said Pooh.

Piglet clung tightly to Pooh. "Is it one of the Fiercer Animals?" he asked in a trembling little voice.

"Yes," said Pooh. "It's a Jagular!"

"What's a Jagular, Pooh?" asked Piglet, as they crept towards the tree.

"Halloooooo," came the howling sound again.

"Jagulars hide in treetops, shouting '*Hallooooo*!'" said Pooh. "And when you look up at them, they drop down on you!"

"I'm looking down, Pooh!" said Piglet quickly. His voice was trembling and his knees were shaking with fear.

"*Hallooooo*!" cried the Jagular again.

Without thinking, Piglet looked straight up at the top of the tree. And what he saw filled him with happy relief.

"Pooh, look!" he cried. "It's not a Jagular at all. It's Tigger, and Roo's up there with him!"

Up in the tree, Roo had spotted their friends below. "Pooh and Piglet are here!" he told Tigger.

"Thank goodness," said Tigger. He was still quite dizzy, and he was beginning to feel very frightened. "Halloo, down there!"

"Hello, Tigger and Roo," called Pooh. "What are you doing up there?"

"We were just doing some bouncing," said Roo, "and Tigger decided to bounce up into this tree. Now he's stuck!"

Tigger in Trouble

"Somebody, please help me!" called Tigger. He was getting more frightened by the minute.

"Don't worry, Tigger," said Pooh. "I'll go and fetch Christopher Robin. He'll know what to do. He always does."

"And I'll stay here and keep you company till they get back," said Piglet. "Gosh, Tigger, I'm glad it's you up there, and not a Jagular! I don't think I would like Jagulars one little bit."

Tigger just groaned.

Pooh ran off as fast as he could, and word soon got round to everyone in the Hundred Acre Wood that Tigger was in trouble. Christopher Robin came running at once, bringing Rabbit and Kanga with him.

Tigger Makes a Promise

"Oh, gracious," said Kanga, when they got to the tree. "Roo, please be careful!"

"I'm all right, Mama," said Roo cheerfully. "But Tigger's stuck!"

"Oh, that's too bad," said Kanga.

"No, that's good!" said Rabbit. "He can't bounce anybody up there!"

"But we have to get him down," said Christopher Robin. He took off his coat and told Rabbit, Kanga and Pooh each to grab a corner. "We'll hold it out like a net," Christopher Robin explained, "and Roo and Tigger can jump into it. You go first, Roo!"

Roo jumped. "Whee!" he cried, bouncing into the coat and out again, and finally landing in Kanga's arms. "That was fun! Come on, Tigger. It doesn't hurt – jump!"

"Jump?" cried Tigger. "Tiggers don't jump – they bounce!"

"Then bounce down," suggested Pooh.

"Don't be ridiculous!" said Tigger. "Tiggers only bounce *up*!"

"Hooray!" cheered Rabbit. "Tigger will have to stay up there for ever!"

"For ever?" groaned Tigger. "Oh, if I can just get down from here, I promise I'll never bounce again!"

"Never?" said Rabbit. "Did everyone hear that? Tigger has promised never to bounce again!"

At last, after much coaxing, a very cautious and timid Tigger let go of the tree.

"There," said Christopher Robin, as Tigger landed safely. "You're all right now."

"I am?" said Tigger. "I am! Oh, thank goodness! I'm so happy I feel like bouncing for joy!"

"Oh, no!" warned Rabbit. "You can't! You made a promise!"

"I did, didn't I?" said Tigger softly. "Does that mean I can't *ever* bounce again?"

"Never!" declared Rabbit.

"Not even one teensy-weensy bounce?" asked Tigger.

"Not even a *smidgen* of a bounce," insisted Rabbit.

Tigger's whole body seemed to sag, and he turned sadly away from his friends.

"You know," said Roo, "I think I like the old, bouncy Tigger best."

"So do I," said Pooh.

Everyone looked at Rabbit.

"Oh, all *right*!" said Rabbit at last. "I like the old Tigger better too!"

Tigger bounced straight at Rabbit. "You mean I can bounce again after all?"

Rabbit nodded.

"Hooray!" shouted Tigger, grabbing Rabbit. "Come on, Long Ears, you bounce with me!"

"Me? Bounce?" sputtered Rabbit.

"Why, certainly!" said Tigger. "After all, you have the feet for it!"

The next thing Rabbit knew, he and Tigger were both bouncing with all their might. And, much to his amazement, Rabbit found that bouncing really *was* wonderful fun – it felt like flying!

Soon everyone was bouncing in the snow, having a perfectly lovely time.

Christopher Robin and his friends never forgot that exciting winter day in the Hundred Acre Wood.

And although Tigger never stopped bouncing, from that day on he was very careful not to bounce near trees!

Grown-ups think that all these stories are make-believe, and that Christopher Robin's friends are just stuffed toys. But you and I know better, don't we?

Of course we do – as sure as there's a Hundred Acre Wood!